TIDY

Emily Gravett

TWO HOOTS

Deep in the forest lived a badger called Pete
Who tidied and cleaned and kept everything neat.

He tidied the flowers by checking each patch,
And snipping off any that didn't quite match.

He tidied the fox by grooming his fur,
He untangled each knot
and each twig and each burr.

He tidied the birds,
from the big to the small,
By brushing their beaks
and then bathing them all.

He picked up stray sticks,
he swept and he rubbed,

He polished the rocks,
and he scoured and he scrubbed.

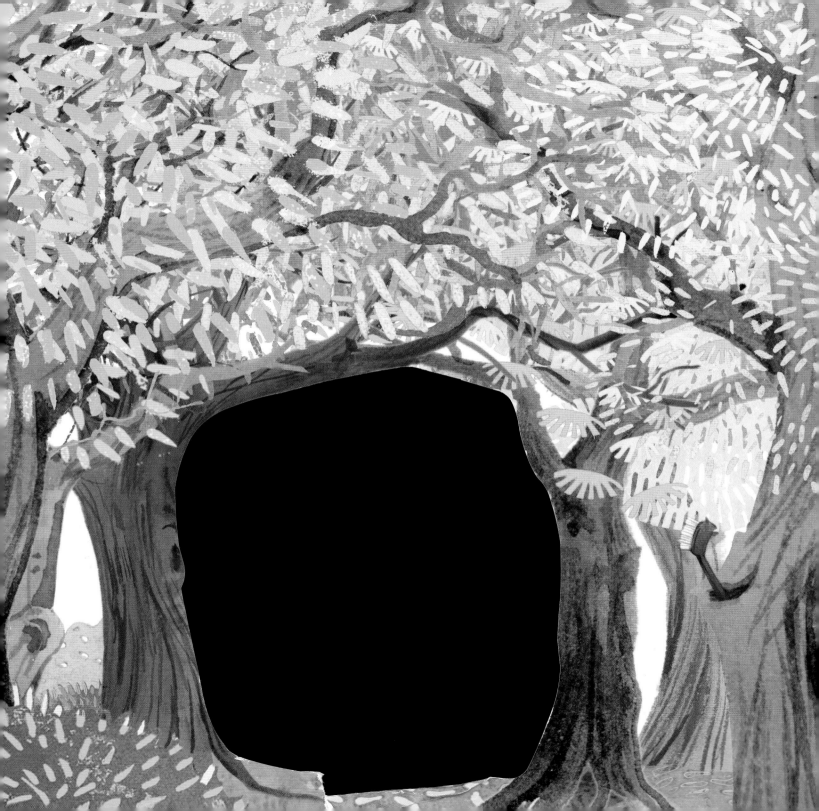

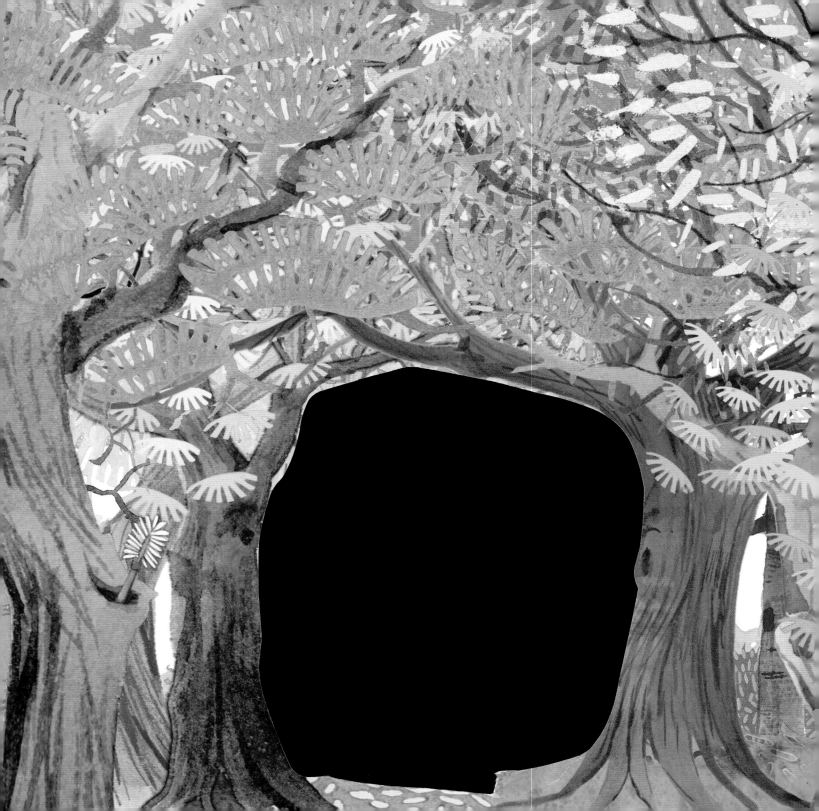

So when a leaf fell,

well . . .

Pete tidied up.

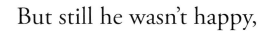

But still he wasn't happy,

Now the trees looked bare and scrappy.

And so, to make it all look neat,

Pete undertook a MIGHTY feat . . .

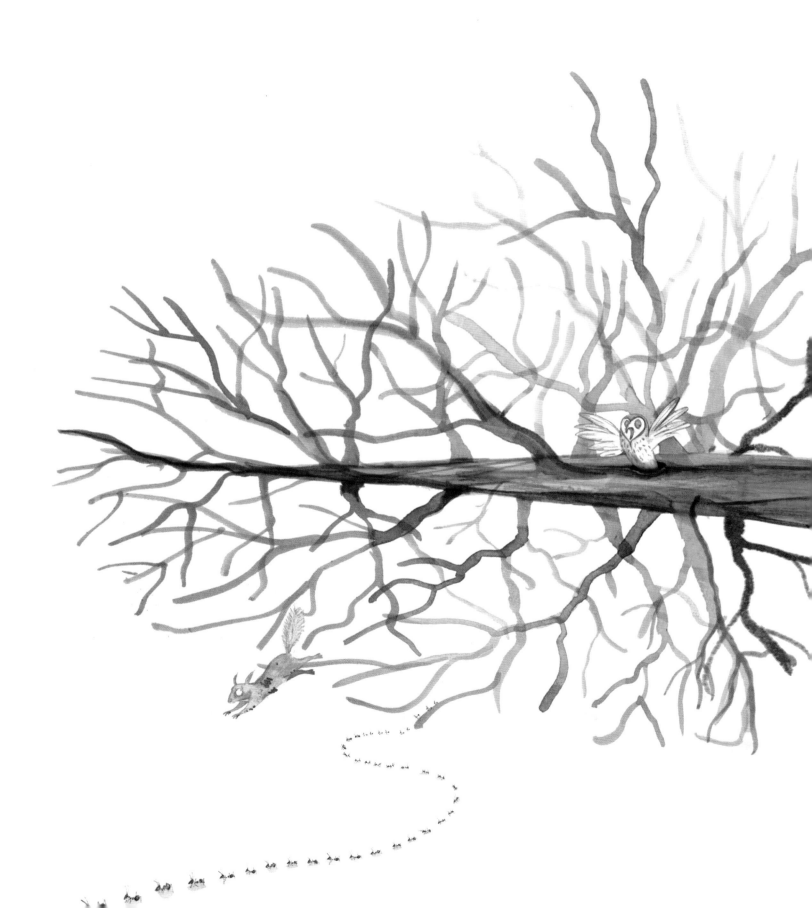

He dug up

every

single

tree!

But then it rained.

There was a

FLOOD!

And afterwards a LOT of

MUD!

Pete called in the diggers,
He called in the mixers,

He called in the concrete,
The rakers, the fixers.

No mud

No leaves

No mess

No trees.

Perfectly tidy and perfectly neat.

"This forest is practically perfect," said Pete.

"I'm hungry!" he thought. "I deserve a treat."
So he hunted around for something to eat.

But the beetles and worms that he usually found
Were under the concrete, deep in the ground.

And so Pete decided to go home instead,
If he couldn't have dinner, he'd go straight to bed.

But when he arrived and took out his key,
There wasn't a door where the door used to be!

Later that night, Pete tossed and he turned.
His belly was empty, it rumbled and churned.

As he lay in his mixer, wide, wide awake
He started to think, "I have made a mistake!"

So . . .

The very next morning, when it got light,
He set about trying to put everything right.

Then the animals came – from the strong to the weak,
And they lent him a paw, or a claw, or a beak.

They put everything back, as it always had been
(But maybe less ordered – and not quite as clean).

And Pete? Well, he promised to tidy up less.
But if he succeeded is anyone's guess!

Keep Your
Forest
Tidy!

For Pat and Grace

First published 2016 by Two Hoots
This edition published 2018 by Two Hoots, an imprint of Pan Macmillan
20 New Wharf Road, London N1 9RR
Associated companies throughout the world
www.panmacmillan.com
ISBN 978-1-5098-8012-6
Text and illustrations copyright © Emily Gravett 2016
Recording copyright © Two Hoots 2018

1 3 5 7 9 8 6 4 2
Printed in China
Read by Lenny Henry
Recorded at Strathmore Publishing
Produced by Elspeth McPherson
Music composed by Jordan Killiard
The illustrations in this book were created using watercolour,
acrylic, wax crayons, linocut and a lot of mess.
www.twohootsbooks.com
A CIP catalogue record for this book is available from the British Library.